For my wonders, Ava, Ricky, Maria, and Rich,
and for our parents and teachers who open us
to a world of wonders. —M.C.L.

For Margaux, Imogen, Isabelle, Alexandre
and Remi with love. —S.I.

Philomel Books 💗 An Imprint of Penguin Group (USA) Inc.

You Are My Wonders

Maryann Cusimano Love

illustrated by Satomi Ichikawa

I am your teacher;
you are my school child.

I am your welcome;

    you are my running wild.

I am your bell;

you are my ring.

I am your notes;

  you are my sing.

I am your tall;
you are my grow.
I am your tell;
you are my show.

I am your blank paper;
    you are my work of art.
        I am your lace doily;
            you are my glitter heart.

I am your go slow;
you are my double-quick.
I am your glue;
you are my Popsicle stick.

I am your story;

   you are my wide eyes.

     I am your lesson;

        you are my surprise.

I am your stillness;
you are my jiggle.
I am your straight line;
you are my wiggle.

I am your serious;

you are my silly face.

I am your duck, duck, goose;
you are my chase.

I am your soil;

you are my watering spout.

I am your seeds;

you are my fresh green sprout.

I am your blackboard;
you are my clean eraser.
I am your chore chart;
you are my hamster chaser.

I am your boots;
you are my muddy tracks.
I am your zip up;
you are my backpack.

I am your calm;
you are my thunder.

I am your wisdom;
you are my wonders.

PHILOMEL BOOKS

A division of Penguin Young Readers Group.   Published by The Penguin Group.
Penguin Group (USA) Inc., 375 Hudson Street, New York, NY 10014, U.S.A.
Penguin Group (Canada), 90 Eglinton Avenue East, Suite 700, Toronto, Ontario M4P 2Y3, Canada
(a division of Pearson Penguin Canada Inc.).
Penguin Books Ltd, 80 Strand, London WC2R 0RL, England.
Penguin Ireland, 25 St. Stephen's Green, Dublin 2, Ireland (a division of Penguin Books Ltd).
Penguin Group (Australia), 250 Camberwell Road, Camberwell, Victoria 3124, Australia
(a division of Pearson Australia Group Pty Ltd).
Penguin Books India Pvt Ltd, 11 Community Centre, Panchsheel Park, New Delhi - 110 017, India.
Penguin Group (NZ), 67 Apollo Drive, Rosedale, Auckland 0632, New Zealand (a division of Pearson New Zealand Ltd).
Penguin Books (South Africa) (Pty) Ltd, 24 Sturdee Avenue, Rosebank, Johannesburg 2196, South Africa.
Penguin Books Ltd, Registered Offices: 80 Strand, London WC2R 0RL, England.

Edited by Michael Green.   Design by Semadar Megged.   Text set in 23-point Zapf Humanist 601 BT.
The art for this book was painted in watercolor on Fabriano paper.

Library of Congress Cataloging-in-Publication Data
Cusimano, Maryann K.   You are my wonders / Maryann Cusimano Love ; illustrated by Satomi Ichikawa.   p. cm.
Summary: Illustrations and rhyming text combine in a celebration of the relationship between teacher and student.
[1. Teachers—Fiction. 2. Schools—Fiction.] I. Ichikawa, Satomi, ill. II. Title.   PZ8.3.C965Yw 2012   [E]—dc23   2011027120
ISBN 978-0-399-25293-8
1 3 5 7 9 10 8 6 4 2